W. H. St. John Hope, Harold Brakspear

Haghmond Abbey

W. H. St. John Hope, Harold Brakspear

Haghmond Abbey

ISBN/EAN: 9783337059767

Printed in Europe, USA, Canada, Australia, Japan

Cover: Foto ©Raphael Reischuk / pixelio.de

More available books at **www.hansebooks.com**

HAUGHMOND ABBEY

By

W. H. St. John Hope

&

Harold Brakspear

From

Archaeological Journal
1909
Volume LXVI

HAUGHMOND ABBEY, SHROPSHIRE.[1]

By W. H. ST. JOHN HOPE, M.A. and HAROLD BRAKSPEAR, F.S.A.

The abbey of Haughmond was built upon the western slope of the hill of the same name, some four miles to the north-east of Shrewsbury. The ruins are remarkably picturesque, and deserve as much attention from the architect as from the archaeologist.

The late Rev. Mackenzie Walcott included Haughmond in his *Four Minsters round the Wrekin*, accompanied by a plan which requires considerable ingenuity to identify.

Some years ago a little excavation was done upon the site of the church, which resulted in the discovery of a porch upon the north side and an altar in a peculiar position beneath the crossing.

Towards the end of 1906 it was felt that the time had arrived to publish an accurate plan of the abbey, but before that was possible a considerable amount of excavation was necessary. Our member, Mr. H. R. H. Southam, after obtaining the necessary leave of the owner, Mr. Hugh Corbett, raised a fund by local subscriptions and grants from the Society of Antiquaries and the Royal Archaeological Institute to enable this work to be done. At Easter of 1907 operations were begun under the directions of the writers and were continued for some weeks.

According to an account given by Tanner in his *Notitia Monastica*,[2] following an erroneous statement in the earliest[3] and later editions of Dugdale's *Monasticon Anglicanum*,[4] " William FitzAlan of Clun, A.D. 1110, founded here an abbey for regular canons of the order

[1] Read before the Institute, 7th April, 1909.

[2] T. Tanner, *Notitia Monastica* (London, 1744; also ed. J. Nasmith, Cambridge, 1787), s.v. Shropshire, xii, Haghmon.

[3] London, 1661, ii, 46.

[4] Ed. Caley, Ellis, and Bandinel (London, 1830), vi, part i, 107.

of St. Augustine, which was dedicated to St. John the Apostle and Evangelist."

Tanner is, however, careful to note that the date 1110 " was before these canons were brought into England," and the Rev. R. W. Eyton, in his *Antiquities of Shropshire*,[1] has also shown that the statement in question, though contained in a cartulary of the abbey, has no foundation in fact. Mr. Eyton also points out that the oldest deed relating to the house is a grant by William FitzAlan of a fishery at Upton-on-Severn, " for the maintenance of Fulco the prior and all his brethren, living in the aforesaid church." From internal evidence Mr. Eyton dates this deed to 1130—1138. He also concludes from it that the house was at first a priory, and afterwards raised to the dignity of an abbey, but it is quite possible that the grant was made during a vacancy in the abbacy, and that the house was an abbey from the beginning. The first benefactors, according to the same authority, included the empress Maud, king Henry II, Walkelin Maminot, William Peverel of Dover, and others, together with Ralph Gernon, earl of Chester, and Walter, bishop of Chester, who died in 1159.

Between 1155 and 1160 king Henry II granted to the canons of Haughmond the seat and place (*ipsam sedem et locum*) of the abbey, together with sixty acres of land which they had assarted, and three plough-lands in Walcot given to them by the empress Maud.[2]

In 1172 pope Alexander III granted to the abbey a bull exempting all the cultivated lands of the canons from payment of tithe, and giving them the right of free burial within the abbey, so operating as to make it extra-parochial.[3]

This parochial independence was completed by Richard, bishop of Coventry (1161-1182), who allowed the sacrist to administer the sacrament of baptism to jews and infants within the monastery, and to act as parish priest to all servants of the house as regarded the administration of the sacraments in general.[4]

---

[1] London, 1858, vii, 283 et seq.
[2] Eyton, vii, 291.
[3] The text of the bull is printed in the *Monasticon* (vi, part i, 112-3).
[4] Eyton, vii, 292.

Several other documents of interest relating to the abbey may also be mentioned. In 1332 abbot Nicholas of Longnor, in consideration of the increased means of the house, granted to the prior and convent (*inter alia*) " that they may have from henceforth a new kitchen assigned for the frater, which we will cause to be built with all speed ; in which they may cause to be prepared by their special cook such food as pertains to the kitchen of that which shall be served to them, every day, by the canons and ministers appointed to that end by them by leave of the abbot."[1] The abbot also grants that " at any time of the year they may have in common the piggery of the house which is without the gate, and twenty pigs at the common cost of the house, for furnishing their larder."[2]

In 1459 an agreement was entered into between abbot Richard Burnell in full chapter, with the assent of his convent, as to the recognitions and observances in his absence due to the prior and subprior. After reciting these the document directs " that the aforesaid claustral prior shall have for his refreshment a certain chamber under the dorter, having an entry in the cloister beside the parlour door, which our beloved brother and fellow canon Dan William of Shrewsbury, now and long before claustral prior, lately repaired at great cost and renewed with many labours, together with a garden called of old Longenor's garden, annexed to the aforewritten chamber, with a dovecot in the same ; all which and singular we grant by these presents to the aforesaid Dan William of Shrewsbury, prior, for his lifetime. And the oft-said claustral prior shall possess the aforesaid chamber with the above-written things, after the death only of the aforenamed William of Shrewsbury, now prior, and all and singular the jewels and ornaments belonging both

---

[1] " Quod iidem prior et conventus habeant de caetero novam coquinam, pro refectorio assignatam, quam aedificari celeriter faciemus ; in qua parari faciant per coquum eorum specialem, cibaria eorum quae ad coquinam pertinent, de quibus ministrabitur eisdem, diebus singulis, per canonicos et ministros ad hoc per eos, cum abbatis licentia deputandos."—*Monasticon*, vi, part i, 111.

[2] " Concedimus etiam pro nobis et successoribus nostris, quod omni tempore anni habeant in communi porcariam domus quae est extra portam, viginti porcos ad sumptus communes domus, pro eorum lardaria faciendo." *Ibid.*

to the altar in St. Andrew's chapel in the church and to the said chamber, etc."[1]

Another altar in the church, that of St. Anne, is mentioned in 1476 in connexion with the foundation thereat of a chantry by John le Strange, lord of Knockin, and Jacinth his wife.[2]

The abbey of Haughmond was suppressed with the larger religious houses in 1539, the so-called surrender, which is signed by the abbot, the prior, and nine other canons, being dated 9th September of that year. The estimated annual value was then £294 12s. 9d.

The site was granted, on 25th September, 1541, to Sir Edward Littleton of Pillaton, in the county of Stafford. He sold it to Sir Rowland Hill, and it passed through his sister to the Barker family. From them it descended to the Kynastons, and in 1740 it came to the family of the present owner.

The precinct of all monastic houses was enclosed by a wall or ditch, but at Haughmond nothing remains to show the extent of the enclosure, though the site of the gate-house can be traced some 400 feet to the north of the church. Between the gate and church was the outer court of the abbey, originally containing numerous buildings necessary to the convent and its guests, but of these no trace remains above ground.

The chief buildings of the abbey are grouped as usual around the cloister, and there is a second court to the south. A peculiarity of the buildings, owing to the site being upon a hill-side, is that some of those upon the highest part have floors quarried out of the red sandstone rock which forms the hill, and the rock itself is left as high as it stood to form the lower parts of the walls.

---

[1] " Inprimis, quod praefatus prior claustralis habebit pro recreationibus suis cameram quandam sub dormitorio, introitum habentem in claustro juxta parlarii ostium, quam praedilectus confrater noster et canonicus dominus Willelmus Salop. pro nunc, et diu ante, prior claustralis nuper magnis reparavit sumptibus et plurimis renovavit laboribus, cum gardino vocato ab antiquo Longenores-gardine camerae praescriptae annexo, una cum columbari in eodem; quae omnia et singula praedicto praefato domino Willelmo Salop. priori concedimus, vita sibi comitante, per praesentes; possidebitque saepefatus prior claustralis cameram antedictam, cum suprascriptis, post decessum solum praenominati Willelmi Salop. nunc prioris, ac omnia et singula jocalia et ornamenta, tam altari in capella sancti Andreae in ecclesia, quam dictae camerae pertinentia, etc."—*Monasticon*, vi, part i, 112.

[2] Eyton, vii, 303.

PLATE I.

To face page 285.

WEST PROCESSIONAL DOORWAY.

All that was standing above ground before our excavations was the western procession doorway to the church, the west front of the chapter-house, the west wall of the cloister, the west end and part of the south side of the frater, and the great hall of the infirmary, with a two-storied block in connexion.

In the buildings of regular canons no system of plan was followed save that the church, chapter-house and frater bore their usual relative positions to each other.

From their first foundation the larger houses had churches of a fully developed plan, as Smithfield, Christchurch, Carlisle, Waltham, Worksop, Bridlington, all of which were aisled in presbytery and nave and had eastern chapels to the transepts. By far the larger number of canons' houses, however, had, in the first place, churches without aisles either to the presbytery or nave, but with two or more chapels to the transepts, as at Lanercost, Bolton, Dorchester, Newstead, Newark, Wigmore, and Lilleshall. In nearly all cases these aisleless churches seem to have been inconvenient, and an aisle was added upon the side away from the cloister.

THE CHURCH.

The canons at Haughmond began their first church upon modest lines, and some of this still remains beneath the floor level of the later work. It consisted of a presbytery, and north and south transepts with one eastern chapel to each, and an aisleless nave was intended to follow. The presbytery was 20 feet 6 inches wide, but its length is uncertain owing to the east end being on the rock ; it had an archway on either side into the transept chapels. These archways were 7 feet 6 inches wide and of two square members ; the east jamb remains of that on the south, and both jambs of the northern arch. Of the crossing both responds of the northern arch remain bedded in later work, and are similar to the jambs of the arches to the transepts. There were no responds to take the east and west arches, which must therefore have been carried on corbels. The north chapel was 11 feet 2 inches wide by 11 feet 5 inches from east to west. The east

wall was unearthed in the previous excavation mentioned
above, and has in it a two-membered recess, 6 feet wide,
for the altar. The altar was 3 feet 4 inches in length,
and in connexion therewith is a floor drain, having a dish
7 inches square, placed diagonally against the jamb of
the arch to the presbytery. Of the corresponding chapel
on the south, the east wall alone remains, but without a
recess for the altar ; it had a chamfered plinth externally.
Search was made for other parts of this original building,
but nothing was found except the rough foundations of
the south-west pier of the crossing, and it is doubtful
if anything further westward was ever built in stone
before it was decided to build the new church and monastery
upon a much larger scale.

The new church was of the aisleless type, very similar
to that of the neighbouring house of Lilleshall, and consisted of a presbytery, north and south transepts with
two eastern chapels to each, and a nave without aisles. As
in the case of the Cistercian foundations of Waverley
and Tintern, it was built to the east and north of the
first church, so that the convent should not be disturbed
in their old quire before the new one was ready for use.
This church was exactly 200 feet in length, and had a
tower over the crossing, under which and the first bay
of the nave was the quire. An unusual feature, owing
to the slope of the ground, must have been the great
number of steps between the nave and the high altar, as
the quire was 6 feet above the nave and the platform
of the high altar 5 feet 6 inches above the quire. In
the early part of the thirteenth century an aisle was
added on the north side of the nave with a large porch
of entrance. At some period before the suppression, the
north transept with its chapels was destroyed, presumably
by the fall of the steeple, after which an aisle was added
to the north of the presbytery with a solid return wall
to form the east side of the transept.

The presbytery was 51 feet in length by 25 feet in
width. Its east wall has disappeared, except its rough
bed quarried in the rock. The north wall, save for a
small piece at the extreme east end, has also completely
gone. The south wall shows in places to a couple of
feet in height as part of the solid rock, and was thickly

PLATE II.

To face page 287.

WEST PROCESSIONAL DOORWAY, WITH FIGURE OF ST. PETER.

coated with plaster. A fragment of the external plinth remains.

There was a cross step at 12 feet and another at 24 feet 6 inches from the east wall. Between these, in the floor, are two grave slabs, of the thirteenth century, having an incised cross upon each with inscriptions round the edge. That to the north is :

+ WOVS · KI· P | ASSEZ · P [AR· IC] I · PRIES · PVR· LALME · IOHAN ·
FIS · | ALEIN · KI · | GIT · ICI · DEV · DE · SA · ALME · EIT ·
MERCI . AMEN.[1]

and that to the south :

+ ISABEL | · DE · MO [RTIME] R · SA · FEMME · ACOST · |
DE · L | VI · | DEV ·] DE · LVR · AL [ME · EIT ·] MERCI · AMEN.

These slabs were found in 1811, and are well figured in *The Gentleman's Magazine* for June, 1825,[2] at which time they were lying in pieces in the chapter-house.

The added aisle on the north side of the presbytery was 13 feet wide, and stopped short of the main east end some 13 feet. Against the middle of its outer wall is a grave. At the west end the aisle wall returns northward to form the east side of the transept, but slightly westward of the line of the original east wall.

Nothing whatever remains of the first or later north transept, owing doubtless to the occurrence of a fault in the rock, necessitating built foundations, which formed a tempting quarry for the destroyers after the suppression.

The crossing had the north, south, and west arches carried upon responds and the east arch upon corbels, but only the footing of the south-east pier, neatly cut in the rock, and the foundations of the south-west pier remain. There would be screen walls under the western part of the side arches, behind the quire stalls, and six or seven steps would lead up to the presbytery.

The south transept was 26 feet wide by 30 feet from north to south, and retains the outer face of the west wall towards the cloister and the foundations, 7 feet

---

[1] This John FitzAlan was born in 1246; he was fourth in descent from the founder, and his wife was daughter of Roger Mortimer of Wigmore, who married Ralph of Arden, 1283, and Robert of Hastings, 1285.

[2] Vol. 95, part i, 497.

9 inches wide, of the south end. The east side was cut into the rock, and the two chapels were gained by a number of steps equal to those up to the presbytery.

Each chapel opened from the transept by an archway of two square members, of which the plinth of the middle pier remains towards both chapels. The northern chapel was 23 feet 6 inches long by 12 feet wide, and the lower parts of its east and south walls remain. The southern chapel was only 11 feet from east to west, though of the same width as its companion.

The nave was about 112 feet long by 26 feet 6 inches wide. The south wall, next the cloister, remains a few feet in height for most of its length, but towards the west it is higher. At its east end are the two northern crossing piers of the first church, with part of the blocking wall between. Through the latter was pierced the eastern procession doorway of the later church. This had five members towards the cloister, of which three were carried by jamb-shafts, and the base of one yet remains on the east side. Towards the church there seems to have been a rere-arch of two members, of which the inner had jamb-shafts.

Westward of the old north-west crossing pier the wall is entirely of the second date, with a small chamfered plinth inside and out. The inner plinth, at 5 feet 6 inches from the old pier, is dropped in three steps to the lower level of the rest of the nave.

The western processional doorway is opposite the west walk of the cloister, and remains complete. It is round-headed, of four members, two being supported by detached columns in the jambs. The hood-mould is richly carved with leaf work, as are also the capitals of the columns, and the outermost member is ornamented with an unusual form between a zigzag and key pattern on its face and soffit (plates I and II). In the fourteenth century the second member of the jambs was cut back and carved into life-sized figures of St. Peter on the east and St. Paul on the west, over which were inserted ogee-headed canopies. Towards the church the doorway has a plain segmental rere-arch within a tall round-headed arch of a single member, which is supported upon banded jamb-shafts with richly carved capitals. The upper part of the arch has gone, but it was carved and had a hood-mould worked with a lozenge pattern (plate IV).[1]

This, as well as the eastern procession doorway, appears to have been inserted in place of simpler openings, though but little later in date than the wall itself.

The west end of the nave has been destroyed, except for its rough foundation and a few stones of the plinth at the north-west angle, where there seems to have been a vice.

The north wall was taken down, in part at any rate, for the arcade to the added aisle, but had originally, like the south wall, a small chamfered plinth inside and out, of which a fragment remains under the fourth pillar from the west.

The north aisle is 12 feet wide at its east end and 11 feet at the west. Externally it has a plinth of two orders, with pilaster buttresses to mark the bays, of which there were seven. The west end stops 5 feet short of the end of the nave. The five western bays had, towards the nave, an arcade carried upon boldly moulded columns, of which the bases and lowest courses of the fourth and fifth from the west and the plinth of the third remain.

The fifth pillar is octagonal on plan, with concave sides to the cardinal points, wherein were detached columns. It had a moulded base and plinth following the line of the middle pier and columns, set upon an octagonal sub-plinth (plate III, no. 1 and fig. 1). The fourth pillar (plate III, no. 2 and fig. 1), is formed of four half circles set diagonally, with wide fillets, and detached columns to the cardinal points; it has a moulded base and plinth following the pillar above. The third pillar, of which the plinth alone remains, was like the fifth, and doubtless the design of the pillars was alternated throughout.

At the fifth pillar the plinth jumps up to follow the rise of the floor level, but nothing remains to show if there were arches in the two eastern bays.

The porch projects from the fifth bay of the aisle; it is 11 feet 6 inches wide by 13 feet deep, and remains

---

[1] After the suppression this doorway was built up, but showing the two outer members to the cloister, and a new doorway, of a single moulded member, inserted in the wall further east. This was the entrance to a small building, on the site of the church, of which the west wall was found with one stone of the hearth of a fireplace.

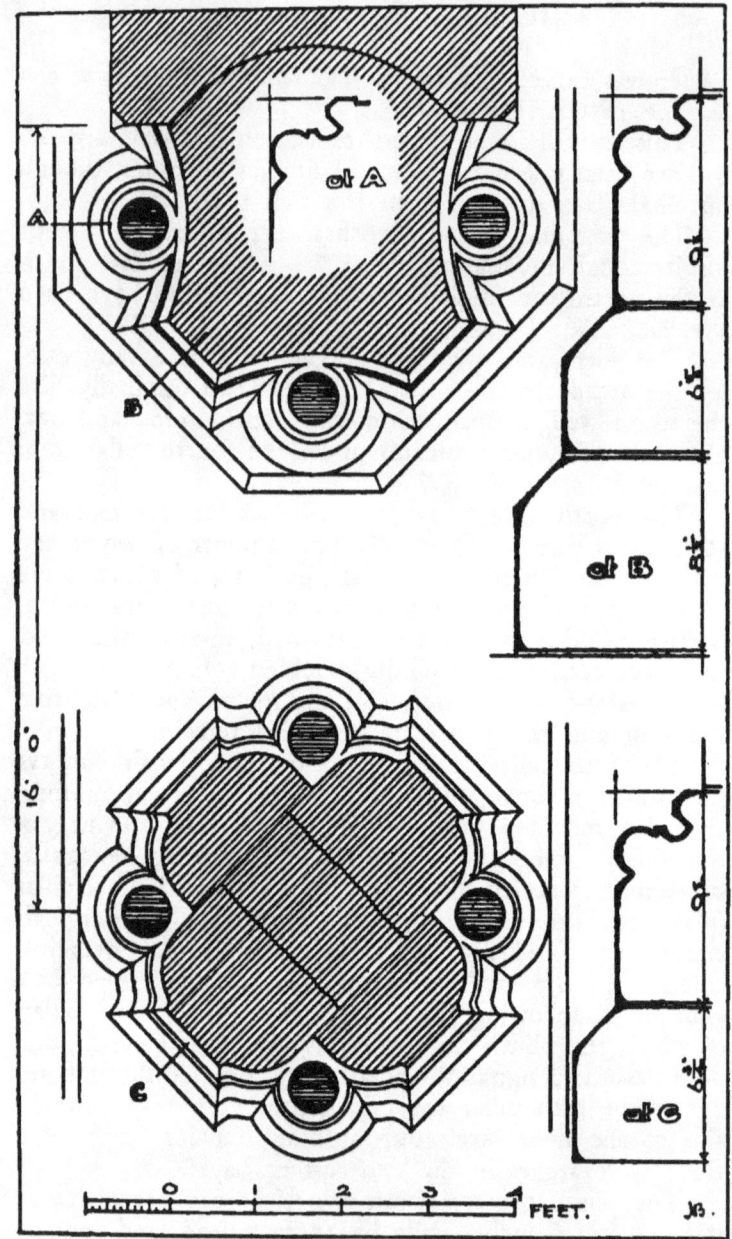

FIG. 1. PLANS OF COLUMNS OF NAVE ARCADE.

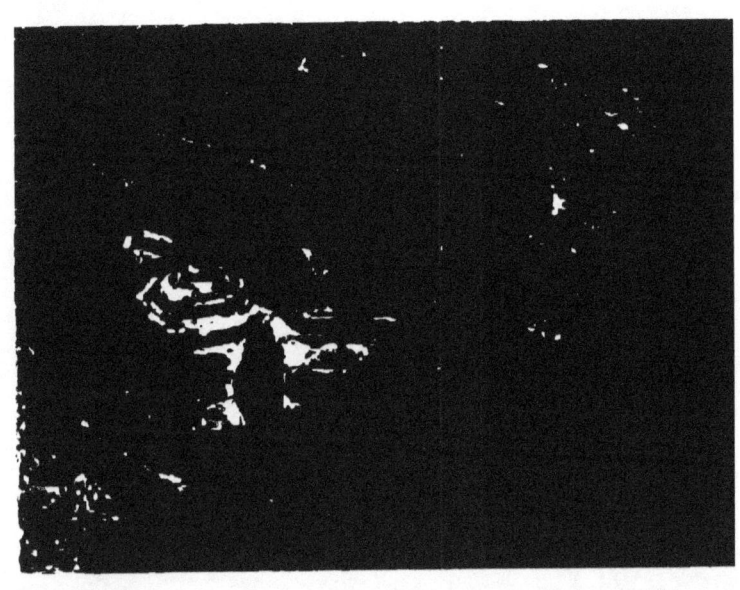

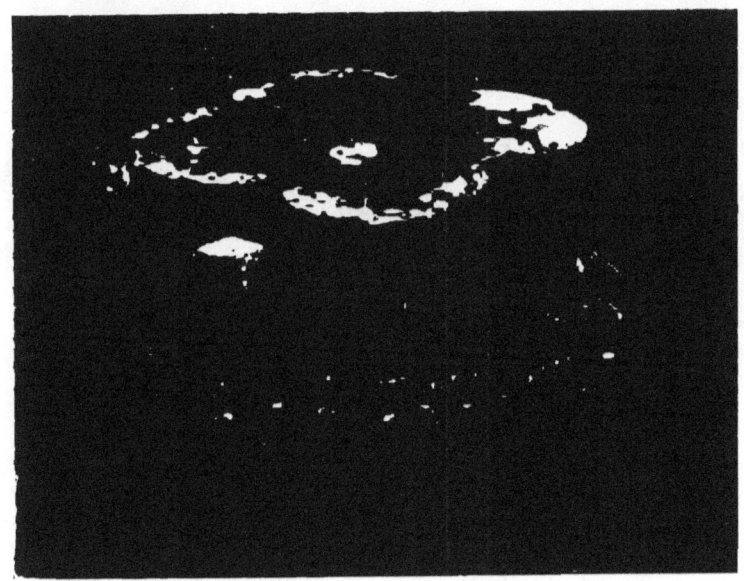

BASES OF PIERS, NAVE ARCADE.

on both sides to about 3 feet in height. The walls have
a plinth similar to that of the aisle, with a pair of pilaster
buttresses at the angles. The outer doorway was of two
members, with a detached column in each jamb. The
inner doorway, of which the bases alone remain, was of
three members, and had four small columns on each side
(fig. 2). There is a sunk space inside the door with two
steps up to the aisle level.

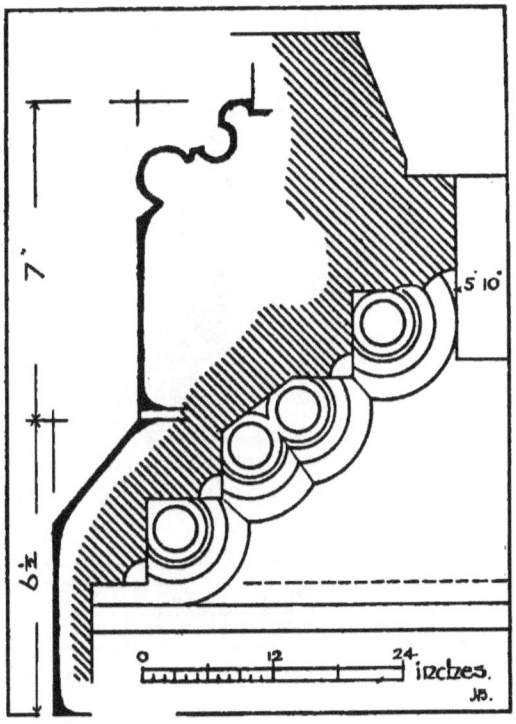

FIG. 2. NORTH PORCH, PLAN OF JAMB AND SECTION OF BASE.

Scarcely anything remains of the internal fittings of
the church, but what is left enables the arrangements
to be made out with a certain degree of accuracy.

The presbytery had the high altar against the east
wall, and its floor was level throughout its length, save
for three cross steps, but was gained by a flight of at
least six steps from the quire.

The quire was also level, 5 feet 6 inches below the presbytery, and occupied the crossing and one bay of the nave, where a cross wall, of which a fragment remains, just within the east jamb of the east processional doorway, enclosed its west end (fig. 3).

There must have been another cross wall to the west of this doorway, and with that to the east, supported the loft or gallery, which formed the *pulpitum*. This always

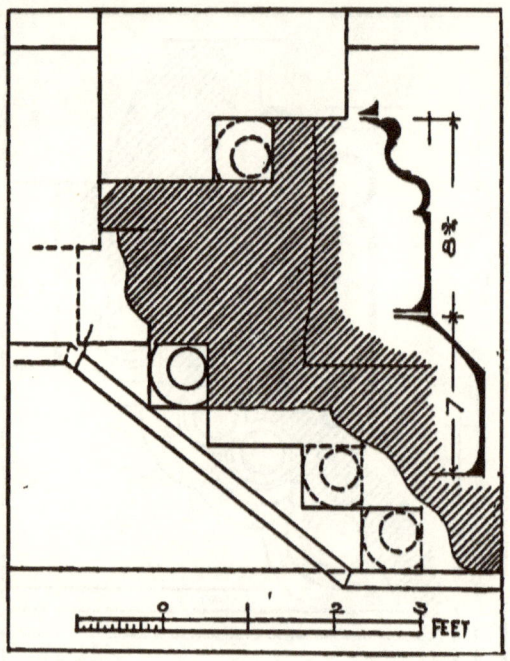

FIG. 3.   EAST PROCESSIONAL DOORWAY, PLAN OF JAMB AND SECTION OF BASE.

divided the quire from the nave in monastic churches, and besides being used for ritual purposes generally held a pair of organs. Against the west side of the *pulpitum*, which also served as the rood screen, was placed the nave altar with a small doorway on either side.

The level of the nave was six feet below the quire, but the original arrangement of steps from the one to the other is not clear. Late in the thirteenth century the nave floor was raised some 6 inches, and a considerable

RERE-ARCH OF WEST PROCESSIONAL DOORWAY.

surface of the paving of this date remains. It has a double row of circular tiles, 12 inches in diameter, down the middle, with a row of square tiles having a narrow tile edging on each side and against the side walls, the general surface being set diagonally with 7 inch tiles, in which, at regular intervals, are circular tiles, like those in the middle. All are much worn, and if they were ever ornamented the patterns are quite lost.

There was a step across the nave 7 feet westward of the easternmost remaining pier of the arcade. Three other steps were at this pillar, with two others to form the platform of the nave altar and up to the doors on each side. On the south side this point is fixed by the level of the processional doorway, from which the level of this quire necessitates a flight of eight steps; these seem to have been placed between the two walls of the *pulpitum*, with a landing in front of the quire door. It is reasonable to suppose that a like arrangement occurred on the north side.

On the west side of the fourth pillar of the arcade are the lower stones of an altar, 4 feet 2 inches in length, which was probably an addition of the fourteenth century; and on the south-west side of the next pillar westward are the foundations of the holy water stock.

In the fifteenth century the nave floor was further raised 15 inches, and the four steps in front of the nave altar removed. Little was found of this floor in position, save a fragment of paving in the north aisle, but in the middle of the nave opposite the third pier of the arcade is a fine incised grave slab (fig. 4). This is 6 feet 2 inches in length by 2 feet 7 inches in width. It has in the middle a figure of a lady with a head-dress of the kind pointed at the top like a ridge of a roof and lappets at the sides over the ears; the dress consists of a tight-fitting bodice with an ornamented collar and a long, flowing skirt; the hands are raised in prayer and gloved, and round the waist is a loose girdle with a buckle of three bosses, from which hangs a long chain of beads. On either side the head is a shield of arms, the dexter is blank, but the other bears a chevron between three lions' heads razed, impaling per fess indented and counterchanged three boars' heads couped.

FIG. 4. INCISED SLAB TO ANKERET, DAUGHTER OF JOHN LEIGHTON, AND WIFE OF RICHARD MYNDE, 1528.

Round the edge is a fine black letter inscription :

𝕳ic 𝕵acet aukerita filia ✠ | 𝕵ohis leiȝton ✱ armig'í
& bror 𝕽icardi mynde ✱ que obiit iu ffe∫to ✱ |
Cathedre Sancti petri | Anno Dñi Mille∫lo CCCCC
rrbiijo cui' aie p[ro]piciet' de[us] am[en].

The first asterisk represents a boar's head couped, the
second a lion's head razed, and the third what looks like
a boot.

In front of the nave altar, on the south side, was found
an interment incased in lead, which doubtless formed the
inner lining of a wooden coffin that had perished ; it
was not thought necessary to interfere with it.

THE CLOISTER.

The cloister is 110 feet from north to south by 93 feet
from east to west. Along each wall was a pentice-covered
alley, 10 feet wide on the east, 10 feet 6 inches wide on
the north and west, and 8 feet 6 inches wide on the south,
supported towards the garth, upon a wall of which the
foundations, 2 feet wide, remain ; they doubtless carried
originally an open arcade upon twin shafts.

The alley next the church was used by the convent
in its leisure time for study, the books for which purpose
were generally kept in a cupboard near the church door.

In the church wall, at 35 feet from the transept, are
the remains of a seat of the thirteenth century, having
projecting jambs with a couple of detached columns in
each, but the lowest course of the west jamb and part of
the back alone remains. A similar seat, in a corresponding
position, remains in the Cistercian houses of Tintern
and Cleeve, and was probably for the use of the claustral
prior to see good order kept.

Adjoining the end of the south transept was a chamber,
11 feet wide, but of uncertain length, of which nothing
remains, but like the similar apartment at Hexham, Oxford,
and Lilleshall, was doubtless the vestry.

THE CHAPTER-HOUSE.

The chapter-house adjoined the vestry southward, and was 26 feet wide, but its length is uncertain. The west end and part of the south side remain to a considerable height, but the north wall is reduced to the foundations, which were traced for 45 feet, and there stop against the rock, in which there is no decided indication of the east end.

The west end is formed by three round-headed arches, of which the middle forms the entrance. It consisted of five moulded members, but the innermost has perished; each member is supported upon a jamb-shaft with carved capitals, and there is an enriched hood-mould with terminals of human heads. The arch on either side has four members, inside of which was a pair of pointed arches carried by twin columns raised upon a sill, 3 feet 6 inches above the floor, but the dividing columns and the stone above are gone (plate v). The southern arch has an enriched label, at the apex of which was a carved head, but that to the northern arch is plainly moulded.

The jamb between the columns have been treated similarly to those of the western processional doorway, but the figures are smaller, and starting from the north are :

On either side of the northern arch : St. Augustine, as an abbot with a crosier, and St. Thomas of Canterbury, with a crossed staff.

On either side of the entrance : St. Katharine with wheel and sword, standing on the crowned head of Maximian, who caused her death ; St. John the Evangelist, with palm branch and scroll ; St. John the Baptist, with the Holy Lamb on a roundel ; St. Margaret, piercing the dragon with her staff (plates vi and vii).

On either side the southern arch : St. Hilda (?) as an abbess, with crosier and book, standing on a head ; and St. Michael, holding a sword, and with his foot on the dragon.

In the north-west angle are the remains of a small corbelled shaft, which is the only evidence that the chapter-house was vaulted, as the south wall seems to have been patched and all evidence of vaulting obliterated.

There remain the jambs of a doorway high up in the

PLATE V.

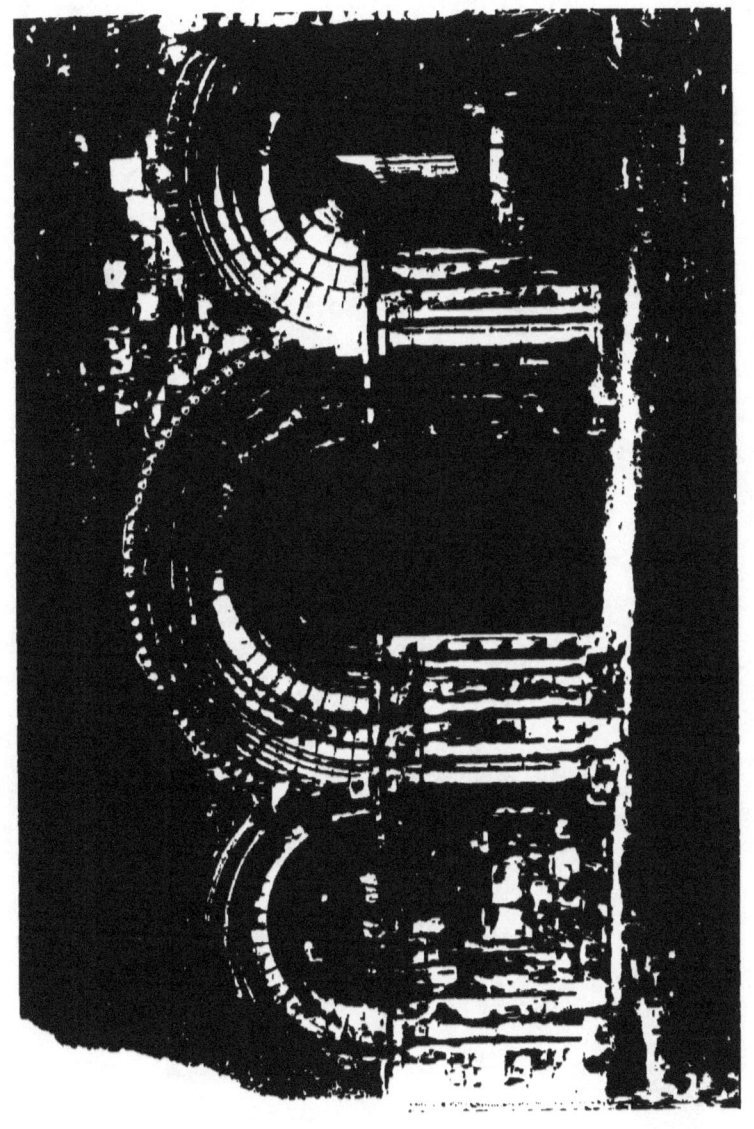

WEST FRONT OF THE CHAPTER-HOUSE.

south wall, which may possibly be monastic, in which case it was to gain access to the church from the dorter by a bridge across the west end of the chapter-house similar to that in the Cistercian abbey of Bindon. After the suppression the chapter-house seems to have been " deemed superfluous," and was, save for the western arches and part of the south side, pulled down. Afterwards the site was again built upon, and a narrow building with semi-octagonal east end erected. It is covered by a heavy oak ceiling, which remains tolerably complete. The east end has square-headed windows removed from elsewhere and a small two-light fifteenth-century window re-used in the north wall. The side openings of the west end were built up, and the entrance narrowed into a doorway, as indicated by the destroyed innermost member. The timber roof is certainly earlier than the suppression, and must have been brought from some destroyed building ; it is divided into four bays, exclusive of the semi-octagonal east end, by heavily moulded beams with a longitudinal beam of similar section, and each compartment is filled with moulded joists.[1]

THE PARLOUR.

Next to the chapter-house was the parlour, but nothing whatever remains of it but the toothing for its east wall.

THE DORTER RANGE.

From the parlour southward, but deflected considerably to the east, was a long two-storied range of building, of which nothing except a fragment of the west wall was visible before the late excavations. The whole area has now been cleared out to its original floor level, and has revealed much of great interest. This building is 125 feet long by 27 feet wide, and was built as a continuous range with a row of columns down the middle dividing it into eleven unequal-sized bays. The columns were 1 foot 8 inches in diameter,

---

[1] This roof was until lately in a grievous condition, and let in the weather, but has now been made secure and weatherproof by the present owner.

with plain chamfered bases, and seem to have merely carried a beam to support the floor above, as they occur opposite original openings. This precludes any regular system of vaulting, by which this building was usually covered.

The east wall is partly formed out of the rock, and thickly plastered internally. In the northernmost bay is a wide recess for a window ; in the next bay a small window recess ; in the third bay an inserted fireplace, 6 feet wide, with a stone curb ; in the fourth bay is part of another wide window recess like that in the first bay ; in the sixth bay the jambs of an original doorway of a single chamfered member ; in the tenth bay was an original window with an inserted mullion ; and in the last bay another original window, with a sink, 18 inches square, recessed in the wall to the south.

The eastern part of the south end remains to some 4 feet in height, and has a doorway of a single square member which led to the subvault of a building which will be described later. The western part of the wall has been demolished, except for the lowest parts, which are formed out of the rock.

The west wall remains in places to a considerable height. Opposite the second column from the north is an original doorway of a single square member.[1] The wall of the fourth and fifth bays has gone, but in the sixth bay are the remains of another doorway opposite to that in the east wall ; in the seventh and ninth bays are the lower internal jamb stones of original windows ; in the tenth bay is an inserted doorway of a single member with a segmental head, which remains complete ; and in the eleventh bay are the lower stones of a similar doorway, though of much smaller opening.

The range has two cross walls parting off the sixth bay as a. passage, presumably of original work. There is another cross wall in the middle of the ninth bay of later date, and against its south side, towards the last, is a raised platform with a chamfered plinth, though for what purpose is not clear. It may have supported a lavatory basin.

The use of the two southern rooms is uncertain, but

[1] This was made into a fireplace in the post-suppression days to warm a room to the west.

IMAGERY ON THE NORTHERN JAMB OF THE CHAPTER-HOUSE ENTRANCE.

that northward of the cross passage was the warming-house, where a fire was kept all through the cold weather, whereat the canons were allowed to warm themselves.

THE PRIOR'S LODGING.

In the first place the warming-house occupied the whole space from the passage to the parlour ; but in the fifteenth century the prior appropriated the northern part

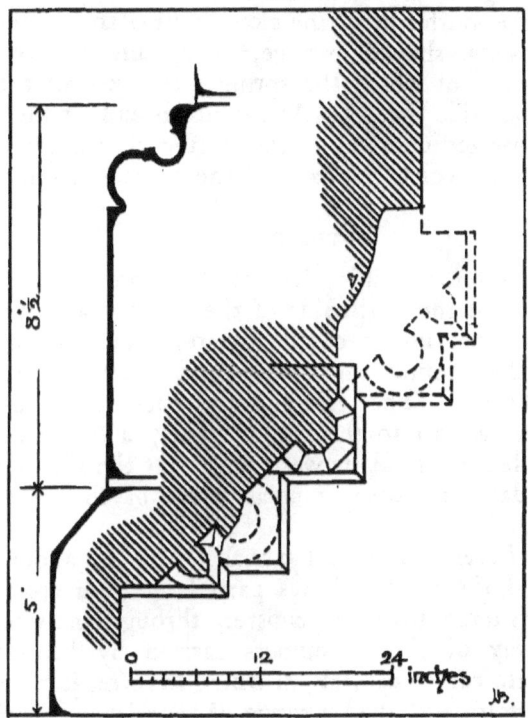

FIG. 5.   THE DARK ENTRY, PLAN OF JAMB AND SECTION OF BASE.

next the parlour to his lodging, and inserted the small doorway of entrance which still remains in the south-east angle of the cloister. He also had a garden for his own use. [1]

THE DORTER.

On the first floor, over the parlour and the whole of the building just described, was the great dorter or sleeping

[1] See page 283 *ante.*

place of the convent. It was approached by steps against
the west side, placed apparently between the warming-
house door and that to the cross passage, and possibly
had a night stair to the church, gained by a gallery across
the west end of the chapter-house.

A monastic dorter was arranged with separate cells or
cubicles made of wood, each lighted by a small window.
They were placed on either side of the range, and had a
wide passage down the middle.

On the south side of the cloister, next the dorter range,
was a wedge-shaped passage,[1] originally covered by a
barrel vault, of which the springer remains for some feet
on the east side (fig. 5). At the north end of the passage
was an inserted doorway of the thirteenth century of three
members, of which the bases of the east jamb remain.

THE FRATER.

The frater, or dining-hall of the canons, occupied the
remainder of the south side of the cloister, and was raised
thereupon by only a couple of steps, but owing to the
fall of the ground southwards and westwards it had a
cellar beneath. The west end and part of the south side
still stand almost to their full height; a fragment of the
north side remains at its west end; but the rest is reduced
to foundations, except a small piece of the core of the
east end.

The frater was 30 feet 6 inches wide by about 81 feet
long, and the west end was parted off by a cross screen.
It was entered from the cloister, through the screens, by
a doorway of three members carried by banded jamb
shafts with carved capitals, of which the west jamb remains.

The south side had a range of round-headed windows,
of which the three western remain. They have wide
splays internally and a continuous hood externally. The
westernmost window is placed in a recess, and has beneath
it the round-headed opening of the service-hatch from
the kitchen placed in a wall arcade of round arches carried
by detached columns with carved capitals (plate VIII).

[1] This was converted into a room at the suppression, having a stone paved floor and a fireplace on the east side inserted into the doorway of the dorter range already named.

PLATE VII.

IMAGERY OF THE SOUTHERN JAMB OF THE CHARTER-HOUSE ENTRANCE.

PLATE VIII.

To face page 301.

SERVING-HATCH AND REMAINS OF WALL-ARCADE, WEST END OF FRATER.

On the west wall this arcade was returned for a short distance, and there are two round-headed lockers to the north. Above were originally three round-headed windows, similar to those on the south side, of which the jambs remain in either angle ; these windows were supplanted in the latter years of the fourteenth century by a large traceried window, transomed at half height, of which the jambs alone remain and have, in line with the transom, a curious band of quatrefoils. The frater floor was of wood carried by cross beams.

The cellar beneath the frater, which was never vaulted, has a wide fourteenth-century doorway inserted in the middle of the west end. It was of two members, with a pointed head, but has lost the inner. On the north side is another wide doorway, with a segmental head, which may be of the original work ; while on the south side is yet another doorway, which has twice been narrowed and is now quite blocked up. In the south wall is a doorway of a single member with a small square-headed loop on the east.

After the suppression the remaining windows of the frater on the south side were built up, and in the cellar beneath a fireplace was inserted in the south wall, and a two-light window inserted close against the west end.

THE LAVATORY.

Just without the frater door, in the west wall of the cloister, was the lavatory where the canons washed themselves in the morning and before going into the frater for meals. It was contained within two round-headed arches, of two square members and a moulded hood, supported upon banded jamb-shafts with beautifully carved capitals. The lower parts of the jambs have been much mutilated, and nothing remains of the basin or any indication of the method by which the water was supplied (plates ix and x). It was one of the duties of the fraterer to see that the lavatory was kept clean and constantly supplied with fresh towels.

THE CELLARIUM.

The west side of the cloister was covered by a range of buildings which, though under the charge of the cellarer and known as the *cellarium* (as in Cistercian houses), was used for quite a different purpose, being for the housing of superior guests.   The east side of the range remains to a considerable height, but the west wall has been destroyed to the foundations.   The north end was partly covered by the church, and the south end was in line with the north wall of the frater, and the toothing for it remains. Although originally of two stories no indication of this is visible.

At the north end of the east wall is a doorway of a single member, with a round rere-arch to the cloister which has jamb-shafts with richly carved capitals.   To the south of this door is an inserted fireplace of the fifteenth century, and yet further south is a small original doorway of a single square member.   The first doorway would indicate that the north end of the range was occupied by the outer parlour.

The *cellarium* was removed, with the exception of its east wall, at the suppression.   Two large buttresses were then built to cover the toothing of the end walls and a battlemented parapet was added to the lowered east wall.

THE KITCHEN.

To the south of the frater is an irregular-shaped court, having the dorter range on the east, the kitchen on the west, and a great hall with a two-storied building on the south.   The west end of the frater is continued southward 86 feet, and against the east side of this wall, which remains in places to a considerable height, was the kitchen and its offices : but without further excavation little about them can be said.

Adjoining the frater must have been a space to contain a staircase up to a lobby outside the serving-hatch.

Southward of this was the great kitchen of the convent, built by abbot Nicholas in 1332 ; it had a fireplace on the west side, and probably others in the destroyed walls. The remaining fireplace is contained in a projecting breast 20 feet 6 inches wide, which is reduced by tabling on either side up to a single flue chimney, but the stack itself has fallen.   High up in the wall, just north of this breast, is an original ogee-headed window.

PLATE IX.

To face page 303.

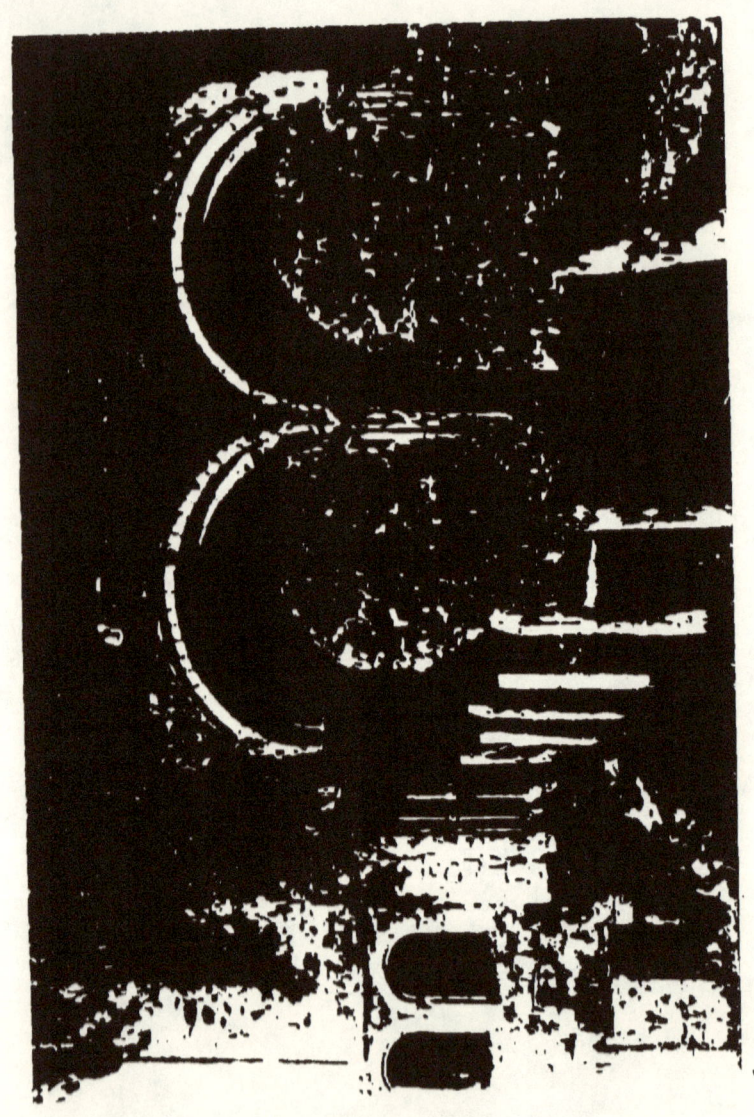

ARCHES OF THE LAVATORY, ON THE WEST SIDE OF THE CLOISTER.

In the continuation of the west wall further south are the remains of another chimney-breast 17 feet wide.

After the suppression the great kitchen seems to have been pulled down, and a new fireplace built further north. Between this and the original breast is a two-light Tudor window, and another of one light was inserted on the north side of the chimney. A new south wall was built at 34 feet from the frater, and in this are remains of a Tudor window like that in the west wall. This kitchen has in turn been destroyed and a little cottage built against the west wall from the frater up to the remaining fragments of the south wall.

On the east side of the court, next the dorter range, was presumably a pentice in continuation with the passage at the east end of the frater. There was certainly a pentice along the south side of the court, which was taken beyond the line of the west wall of the kitchen up to the angle of the hall, where it formed a porch over the chief entrance.

THE INFIRMARY.

The great hall which occupies part of the south side of this second court is set east and west, and stands nearly complete. It is 78 feet 6 inches long by 35 feet wide, roughly divided into four bays, and, with the exception of the east wall, is all of the early part of the fourteenth century. The west end was divided off by screens like an ordinary domestic hall.

The main entrance was at the extreme west end of the north side, 6 feet 6 inches wide, and of two moulded members with a segmental arched head. In the next bay eastward, of the same wall, are the remains of a two-light window placed high up to avoid the roof of the pentice without. In the third bay is an arched doorway of a single moulded member, with indications of another two-light window above. In the easternmost bay is a small pointed doorway, of a single chamfered member, which has in its eastern reveal a straight flight of steps in the thickness of the wall, leading to the first floor of the building on the east. The staircase is lighted on the north side by a small quatrefoil window.

The east end is blank and of an earlier date than the

hall, but has towards its south end two doorways, of which the northern has two members and seems contemporary with the wall, and the southern of one member was inserted when the hall was built.

The south wall has in each bay a two-light transomed window, with tracery still remaining in the head, of which the lower lights are rebated for shutters and the upper grooved for glass (plate xi). There are remains of side seats in the sills of each. In the third bay from the east bay is a pointed doorway leading outwards, and in the west is another doorway leading outwards, but this has been rebated at a later date for a door opening inwards. Externally the bays on this side are separated by bold buttresses, of which the westernmost differs. from the others in having a crocketed gablet to the lower set-off. The walls were originally finished by parapets, and the stone shoots for the rain water still remain to the east of the easternmost and to the west of the westernmost buttress.

The west end (plate xii) has in the middle a pair of pointed doorways leading outwards, with heavy relieving arches, and a small doorway at the north end to a vice in the north-west angle which led up to the parapet. From this vice, at about 14 feet from the ground, is a doorway on to a wall gallery across the west front to another vice in the south-west angle (fig. 6). Above the gallery the wall is thinned, and contains a large window of six lights originally, of which the arch, with pieces of its tracery attached, remains.

Externally the front was covered by a building of which the toothing of its north wall remains, together with four corbels to carry its flat roof, which reached to the sill of the great window (plate xiii). The northern end was raised another story in timber construction, and had a pitched roof placed east and west; it was entered by an inserted doorway in the north-west vice. Search was made for the foundation of these buildings, but nothing decided was found; but from their position and the two doors of entrance from the hall, the ground story was evidently the buttery and pantry of the great hall. The upper part of both turrets containing the vices are turned into circular drums capped by plain pyramidal

PLATE X.

PIER DIVIDING THE ARCHES OF THE LAVATORY RECESS.

PLATE XI.

To face page 305.

WINDOW AND BUTTRESS OF THE INFIRMARY HALL.

tops, and have doorways on to the parapets. The weathering on the east side of both turrets shows that the present gable belongs to a later roof of less pitch than the original one. The southern turret has at the top a second doorway on the south side that led into a building which has been destroyed above ground, but must have been of two or more stories. This was traced by excavation. It was of an earlier date by fifty years than the hall, and

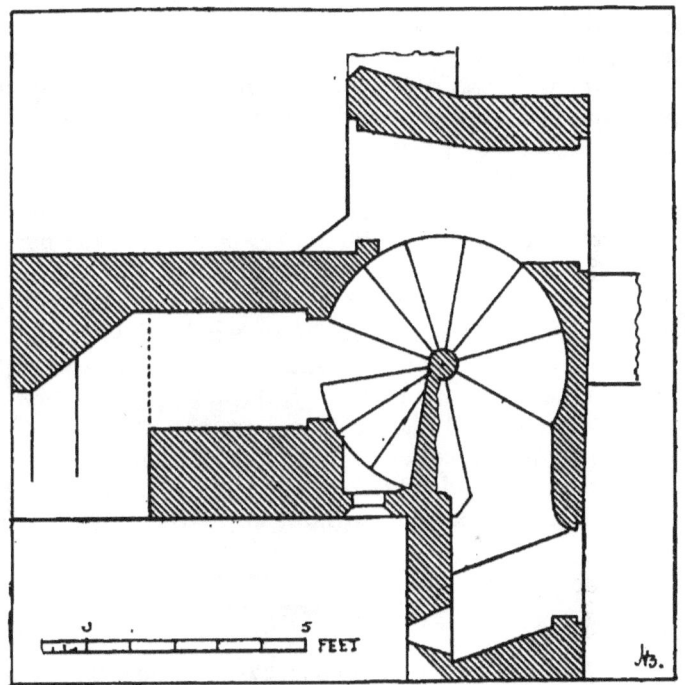

FIG 6.   NORTH WEST CORNER OF INFIRMARY HALL AT FIRST FLOOR LEVEL,
PLAN OF VICE.

placed at a considerable angle thereto. It was 34 feet 6 inches from east to west by 18 feet 6 inches wide, and its north-east corner adjoined the south-west angle of the hall, against which its toothing remains. The floor level of the lowest story was considerably below that of the hall, and had a doorway at the west end of its north side and another at the east end of its south wall, with a narrow loop adjoining. It had a block for a chimney upon an upper floor nearly in the middle of its south wall. It is impossible to say definitely what the use of this building was, but from its character it must have been the lodging of one of the chief officers of the convent, and from its position presumably that of the infirmarer.

Nothing has been said of the use of the hall, but it can hardly have been for any other purpose than that of the infirmary, which, in monastic establishments, was not only for the temporary housing of the sick, but for those who had been professed for fifty years and others who were not able to bear the rigorous life of the cloister. With canons it was also used for the accommodation of those who had been let blood at the fixed periods ordered for this weakening process.

After the suppression it seems to have been used for the hall of the dwelling house. A wide fireplace, having a flat arch with carved spandrels, was inserted in the north wall, and has a large projecting breast externally. A new porch was built to cover the doorway at the west end of the south side, but has been almost wholly destroyed.

In connexion with all monastic infirmaries was a chapel, but of that at Haughmond no sign remains. The doorway on the south side of the hall indicates the existence of a building in that direction, and as it is the only free side, it is there the chapel must be looked for. Trenches were dug for the purpose, but without any satisfactory result.

THE ABBOT'S LODGING.

At the east end of the infirmary hall, and placed roughly at right angles thereto, is a two-storied building, apparently of the thirteenth century, though much altered in later times. It measures 65 feet in length by 21 feet 9 inches in width, and on the ground floor appears to have been divided by a partition into two rooms of almost equal size. In the north wall were originally two narrow windows, of which the eastern is walled up, and the western was altered in the fourteenth century into a pointed doorway of a singled chamfered member. In the south wall are the two doorways from the hall already mentioned, leading into either room ; further south is a small window of

INTERIOR OF WEST END OF INFIRMARY HALL.

the original work, and southward again a wide three-light window of late fourteenth-century date, with a square head. Externally, at the south-west angle, is a large buttress of the same work.

More than half the south end is cut away for the insertion of a large semi-octagonal bay window (plate xiv), having two cinquefoiled lights in each pane, which remains entire. In the remaining piece of wall to the east is a small segmental-headed doorway leading to a contemporary adjunct, which apparently held a stair to the upper floor.

The east side is mostly destroyed, but had in a projecting breast a fireplace to the southern chamber.

Of the upper floor no monastic feature remains, save that in the north-west angle is the opening on the top of the wall stair from the hall, and in the south wall a similar doorway to that below.

The use of this building was doubtless for the abbot; but, owing to its having been so much altered in post-suppression days and having lost most of its east side, the original divisions are obscured. A suggested arrangement is that on the ground floor the northern of the two rooms was the abbot's hall and the southern room with the bay window and fireplace his solar. The destroyed building attached to its south end contained a staircase to the room above the solar, which was the abbot's bedroom. The rest of the upper story was the sleeping place for the infirm, with direct communication with the hall by the wall-stair already described. It should be remembered that the abbot of a canons' house did not require a separate hall of any size, as he was allowed to entertain superior guests in the frater.

The post-suppression alterations were chiefly on the upper floor, and consisted : (1) of raising the added bay to this floor and throwing a pointed arch above to take the gable ; (2) putting a pair of buttresses at the south-east angle to cover the toothing of an adjoining building then demolished ; (3) removing the north end and building a new gable 4 feet 6 inches further north. On the ground floor a fireplace with external breast was inserted in the west wall, and a couple of two-light windows were inserted in the east wall near its north end.

There is a small building filling up the remainder of

the second court between the abbot's lodging and the
dorter range. Its north wall remains, of two dates, and
has a doorway at its west end. The end of its south wall
shows inside the abbot's lodging. It was probably used
on the ground floor as a cellar and above as part of the
sleeping space for the infirmary ; it probably had a small
door into the dorter, by which the servant of the infirmarer
might attend on emergency any canon in the dorter.

THE REREDORTER.

One of the important buildings of the convent has
yet to be described, and that is the reredorter or *necessarium*.
This building was always in direct communication with
the dorter, and was placed so as to be convenient for the
great drain of the abbey. It is sometimes parallel with
the dorter, sometimes at right angles to it, and sometimes
at the end ; but at Haughmond it is in a position to
which there is no known parallel, being placed diagonally
between the south-east angle of the dorter and the corresponding angle of the abbot's lodging.

It is of the same date as the dorter range, 95 feet in
length by 15 feet in width, with a drain 3 feet wide along
its south-east side. The drain channel is only 15 inches
wide, and has battered sides in ashlar courses.

The south end would doubtless have a garderobe on
both stories in connexion with the abbot's lodging, and
he would probably use the passage of the reredorter after
giving the blessing in the dorter at night to retire to his
own chamber.

The reredorter seems to have been pulled down to
the ground after the suppression.

THE CONDUIT.

On the hill side above the reredorter is a small and
simple conduit head of the fourteenth century with a
gabled roof, from which the convent was supplied with
water. The overflow is taken to a small pond, from which
led the main drain, and as the quantity of water is not
sufficient to keep this constantly flushed by a running
stream, the pond was probably let out through a sluice
at stated periods to effect that purpose.

PLATE XIII.

WEST FRONT OF INFIRMARY HALL.

PLATE XIV.

To face page 309.

BAY WINDOW AND BASE OF ORIEL, SOUTH END OF ABBOT'S LODGING.

Most of the features of the post-suppression house have been mentioned where they occur in the earlier buildings; but it may be of interest to state briefly the transformation so far as it can be traced.

The church, chapter-house, cellarer's building, and reredorter were all swept away, except the wall of each building adjoining the cloister, which was retained to enclose a garden.

The infirmary hall was left for the hall of the new house, but a small porch was added to the north door, which became the chief door of entrance to the house. The abbot's lodging was left for the solar below and the great chamber above. The convent kitchen was pulled down, and a new kitchen next the frater was built in its place.

The frater and dorter seem to have been each divided into rooms opening off a long gallery in the same manner as the similar buildings were treated at Lacock in Wiltshire.

A new building, though made up of old material, was built on the site of the chapter-house, apparently for use as a chapel.

A large garden was enclosed to the south and east, by a high wall having a handsome tabled coping of two courses.

We have not been able to find definitely who converted the abbey into a house, but from the character of the work it could only have been done a few years after the suppression. The house was apparently destroyed during the Rebellion, as in the supplement to *The Gentleman's Magazine* for 1790 (p. 1193) it is stated that " In the time of the Civil Wars of the last century, Captain Hosier (I suppose of the Berwick family) burnt the house of Mr. Barker, of Haughmond Abbey, near Shrewsbury, by setting fire to the yule log."[1]

The earliest known view of the abbey is that of S. and N. Buck (1730), which shows the ruins virtually as they are at present, excepting that the east gable of the infirmary hall was then standing, as well as that at the north end of the abbot's house.

Haughmond had a cell, at Ronton in Staffordshire,

---

[1] For this reference the writers have to thank Mr. H. R. H. Southam, F.S.A.

founded by Robert FitzNoel, in the time of Henry II.
The buildings were converted into a house at the suppression. Part of the cloister, of thirteenth-century work
with coupled columns and foliated capitals was standing
until the middle of the last century. The tower at the
west end of the church still stands; it is of the fifteenth
century, and has bold double buttresses at the angles and
a vice at the north-east angle. On the west face is a
doorway of reused thirteenth-century work, beneath a
great window of five lights with a crocketted label; above
is the belfry stage, which has on all four sides a two-light
window and finished with a cornice and battlemented
parapet. Beneath the parapet is a rich band of tracery
work.

On the south side of the tower is a twelfth-century
doorway of a single member, but with a moulded label
which has curious turned terminals no less than 1½ feet
in length and 13 inches high.

www.ingramcontent.com/pod-product-compliance
Lightning Source LLC
Chambersburg PA
CBHW021229260626
47172CB00002B/669